PENGUIN BOOKS
DANCE LIKE A MAN

Mahesh Dattani, born in Bangalore on 7 August 1958, studied in Baldwin's High School and St. Joseph's College of Arts and Science, Bangalore.

He has worked as a copywriter in an advertising firm and subsequently with his father in the family business. His theatre group Playpen was formed in 1984, and he has directed several plays for them, ranging from classical Greek to contemporary works. In 1986, he wrote his first full-length play, *Where There's a Will*, and from 1995, he has been working full-time in theatre. In 1998, he set up his own theatre studio dedicated to training and showcasing new talents in acting, directing and stage writing, the first in the country to focus on new works specifically.

In 1998, Dattani won the Sahitya Akademi award for his book of plays, *Final Solutions and Other Plays*, published by East-West Books, Chennai, thus becoming the first English language playwright to win the award.

Dattani teaches theatre courses at the summer sessions programme of Portland State University, Oregon, USA, and conducts workshops regularly at his studio and elsewhere. He also writes radio plays for BBC Radio 4.

He lives in Bangalore.

# DANCE LIKE A MAN

## A Stage Play in Two Acts

*Mahesh Dattani*

**PENGUIN BOOKS**

An imprint of Penguin Random House

## PENGUIN BOOKS

USA | Canada | UK | Ireland | Australia
New Zealand | India | South Africa | China | Singapore

Penguin Books is part of the Penguin Random House group of companies
whose addresses can be found at global.penguinrandomhouse.com

Published by Penguin Random House India Pvt. Ltd
4th Floor, Capital Tower 1, MG Road,
Gurugram 122 002, Haryana, India

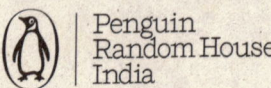

Penguin
Random House
India

First published by Penguin Books India 2006

10 9 8 7 6 5 4 3 2

ISBN 9780143062080

Typeset in Sabon by Mantra Virtual Services, New Delhi

Printed at Repro India Limited

www.penguin.co.in

MIX
Paper from
responsible sources
FSC® C047271

This is a legitimate digitally printed version of the book and therefore might not
have certain extra finishing on the cover.

*Dance Like a Man* was first performed at Chowdiah Memorial Hall, Bangalore, on 22 September 1989, as part of the Deccan Herald Theatre Festival. The cast was as follows:

| | |
|---|---|
| YOUNG JAIRAJ/VISWAS | Mahesh Dattani |
| YOUNG RATNA/LATA | Anjali Jayadev |
| OLD JAIRAJ/AMRITLAL | Vivek Shah |
| OLD RATNA | Dilshad Master |

| | |
|---|---|
| *Director* | Mahesh Dattani |
| *Choreographers* | U.S. Krishna Rao |
| | Chandrabhaga Devi |
| *Incidental music* | Nimesh Patel |
| | Pradeep Narrain |
| *Sets and Lighting* | Pradeep Belawadi |

The play was subsequently performed at the NCPA Experimental Theatre, Mumbai, on 14 February 1990, with Mahesh Dattani, Anjali Jayadev, Vivek Shah and Hema Mandanna, and directed by Mahesh Dattani.

It was also performed by Prime Time in 1995, with Lillette Dubey, Siddhartha Basu, Shivani Wazir and Joy Sengupta, and directed by Lillette Dubey. This production continues to tour occasionally.

# ACT I

*A dimly-lit room in an old-fashioned house in the heart of the city. Up centre is the entrance to the room—a huge arched doorway. There is a rather modern-looking rear panel behind the entrance with a telephone and a modern painting on it. The rear panel can be slid to reveal a garden. Upstage left, a dance practice hall. Upstage right, a staircase going to the bedrooms. Downstage right, exits into the kitchen. All the furniture in the room is at least forty years old.*

*Lata and Viswas enter from the doorway.*

VISWAS. So this is where I get killed.

LATA. They should have been here by now.

VISWAS. They are not in? You said it was all arranged. Wait a minute. They said seven o'clock.

LATA. I know, but they had to go out. Emergency.

VISWAS. Only doctors and firemen go out on emergencies. Dancers stay at home till it's show time. They also stay at home when they have invited their future son-in-law to their house.

LATA. Don't be so sure. They have to meet you first.

VISWAS *(sits down)*. I'm sure they are anxious to get rid of you. We will probably discuss wedding details. You know, things like what they are going to give you, who feeds how many people. Then your mother will want to meet my mother and they'll show each other their Kanchipuram saris.

LATA. Oh, Viswas! Maybe I should throw you out before they come.

VISWAS. But where are they?

LATA. One of our musicians isn't well. He fell down the stairs and broke his arm.

VISWAS. Did he trip on his dhoti or something?

LATA. But they promised they'd be here by seven.

VISWAS. They might still be at the hospital. I can see them now—'Excuse us, we must rush. We have a son-in-law to meet.'

LATA. Don't be under the impression that they are tripping over themselves to meet you.

VISWAS. Why? Aren't they anxious to know who their lovely Lata is marrying?

LATA. Actually they couldn't care less who or what you are. As long as you let me dance.

VISWAS. Hmm. And what if I whisk you away to Dubai and sell you to a sheikh?

LATA. Well, at least I'll still be dancing in his harem! No, seriously, they are not worried.

VISWAS. What kind of parents are they?

LATA *(smiles)*. I told you, they are different.

VISWAS. Did you tell them about my father?

LATA. Yes.

VISWAS. That he runs a mithai shop on Commercial Street?

LATA. Yes. And also that he owns half the buildings on that road.

VISWAS. I hope they don't think they've caught a big one.

LATA. I hope you don't think you've caught a big one.

VISWAS. Why should I think that?

LATA. Simple. I'm the sole heir to this property. It's worth quite a lot.

VISWAS *(looks around)*. This? Quite old-fashioned. High ceiling and all. The wood is probably rotting. But at least it's huge.

LATA. Right in the centre of town. Do you know how much this land is worth? A Marwari builder offered my father ninety lakhs! *(Viswas whistles.)* He wants to build a shopping complex.

VISWAS. So is he selling it?

LATA. No. *(Looks at Viswas.)* He would never do that. My parents have spent all their lives here. My mother's house, I'm told, used to be just five buildings away. There's nobody there now. Even before they married, she used to practically live here. They practised dance together under the same guru. Come on, I'll show you where we practise.

VISWAS. You did tell me it was big but I never expected this.

*Lata leads Viswas to the dance hall and switches on the lights.*

Wow! I've never seen a house like this before.

LATA. Some of these instruments are the same ones my parents used. Almost forty years old. *(Picks up a pair of dancing bells.)* Can you believe it? These are the same bells my father wore for his debut! Ooh! I get goosebumps every time I touch them. This room has something special in it. Can you feel it?

VISWAS. What? The goosebumps?

LATA. Atmosphere! Vibrations! *(Shakes the bells.)*

VISWAS. Yes, that too.

LATA. This floor has felt a million adavus. Over and over again. *(Stamps on the floor.)* Feel that?

VISWAS *(nods)*. I hear it too.

LATA. When I was a little girl, I used to stand near the door and watch mummy and daddy practise. It was magic for me. I knew then what I wanted to be. Viswas, when we are married—you will let me come here to practise, won't you?

VISWAS. Of course, Lata . . .

LATA. Oh, thank you! (*Holds the bells to her eyes and replaces them on the floor.*)

VISWAS. Don't thank me. I don't think our floor can withstand a million adavus.

LATA. And we won't have children.

VISWAS. And we won't have . . . what?

LATA. I mean, not right away. We can have them later, can't we?

VISWAS. My father almost died when I told him I'm marrying outside the caste. Wait till he hears this!

LATA. There's plenty of time. We are still young. (*Comes back to the main room, Viswas follows.*) My parents had me when they were both forty.

VISWAS. Maybe we can adopt one.

LATA. Don't be silly.

VISWAS. We could practise on him, so we would know what to do when our own brat comes along. You know, like a dress rehearsal.

LATA. Do you want children?

VISWAS. Yes.

LATA. Lots and lots of them?

VISWAS. Yes.

LATA. Then go marry someone else!

VISWAS. Oh, Lata, Lata. At least let's settle for two.

LATA *(smiles)*. Okay.

VISWAS. You mean it?

LATA. One child right away and another . . . let's see.

VISWAS. Cheer up. We might get twins. Love's labour saved.

LATA. You are a clown. I don't know what my parents will think of you.

VISWAS *(looks at his watch)*. They have to meet me first.

LATA. Sit down. *(They sit in silence for a while.)* Maybe I should make some coffee for you.

VISWAS. Why maybe?

LATA. I don't know. It's the done thing, isn't it?

VISWAS. Well, if you feel you must, don't let me stop you.

LATA *(gets up and stops)*. On the other hand, I don't have to make it if you don't want it.

VISWAS. But if it's the done thing, then you must.

LATA. Why? There's no one else here except you and me. So who cares whether it's done or not? Unless you have a desperate desire to drink coffee. *(Pause.)* Do you?

VISWAS. Not really.

LATA. Good. That's settled then. *(Sits down.)*

VISWAS. On the other hand, I prefer rattling cups to twiddling thumbs.

LATA. I'll make some. *(Gets up.)*

VISWAS. If it isn't too much of a bother. Actually, I could do without it.

LATA. Do you or do you not want some coffee?

VISWAS. Filtered?

LATA. Instant.

VISWAS. You have tea?

LATA. We don't make tea in this house.

VISWAS. Well, you better get used to making it. Me marrying a Southie my father will tolerate, but accepting a daughter-in-law who doesn't make tea is asking too much of him.

LATA. I'm not a Southie. My father is Gujarati.

VISWAS. Do you have tea in the house?

LATA. No.

VISWAS. Then you're a Southie.

LATA. Fine. I'll get some tea from the shop nearby and . . .

VISWAS. Not just now. I'll let you know when I feel like it, thank you.

LATA (*sighs*). We're not even married yet and I find you exasperating.

VISWAS. Oh, my God!

LATA. Now what?

VISWAS: Your father is a Gujju?

LATA. So?

VISWAS. And he doesn't drink tea?

LATA. Mummy's influence, I suppose.

VISWAS. What a cruel thing to do to a Gujju. Not giving him tea! Your mother must be dominating the poor man!

LATA. I guess daddy is a bit more . . . pliable than usual. Like you.

VISWAS. You think I'm pliable?

LATA. Yes.

VISWAS *(sighs)*. I suppose I am.

LATA. Don't worry. I won't take advantage.

VISWAS. But your mother does.

LATA. Does what?

VISWAS. Dominate. Bully your father.

LATA. No. She does not!

VISWAS. That's a relief. That sort of thing runs in the family, you know.

LATA. That's not true. My grandfather was the dominating type but look at my father, he . . .

VISWAS. Your grandfather? I thought he was dead.

LATA *(with patience)*. He is now. He wasn't before.

VISWAS. You haven't told me much about him.

LATA. He died when I was still a baby. But I know all about him. He was a social reformer. Used to hold secret meetings in this very room during the British Raj.

VISWAS. Oh, a freedom fighter!

LATA. I suppose that was the big cause then.

VISWAS. And after we became free?

LATA. He must have had his hands full handling daddy, what with him wanting to be a dancer!

VISWAS. They must have had some terrific fights.

LATA. They must have. But daddy has always had a deep respect for him. That's why he will never sell this house. Do you know most of the furniture in this room is my grandfather's? My father refused to part with any of it.

VISWAS. That's it!

LATA. Huh?

VISWAS. So that's what it is.

LATA. What?

VISWAS. This room reminded me of something. Now I know what. An antique shop.

LATA. Well, everything here is at least forty or fifty years old.

VISWAS. Over here. *(Moves towards the doorway.)* But in the living room, everything is quite new.

LATA. That wasn't there before. This was the living room. There was a huge lawn in front. My mother had the front extended. We allow very few people to come right in. Only musicians and dancers. The others we finish off with in the living room.

VISWAS. I'm not a musician or a dancer, why didn't you finish off with me in the living room?

LATA. You are part of the family.

VISWAS. Not yet. I still have to approve of your parents.

LATA. What has happened to them? Sit down. I'll call Muthiah, our flutist, and find out where they are. *(Makes to go to the living room.)*

VISWAS. Where are you going?

LATA. To use the phone.

VISWAS *(points to an old-fashioned phone)*. What's wrong with this one?

LATA. That's also part of the antique show. It's a dummy, dummy. *(Goes to the living room.)*

VISWAS *(looks around the room and shakes his head).* I'm going to get in-laws who are ready for the nut house!

*While Lata is on the phone, Viswas looks around the room. He is intrigued by a large ornate cupboard.*

LATA. Hello. Muthu uncle? Lata here. Yes. I'm fine, fine . . . No, they are not back. That's why I called to find out . . . Oh, that's too bad. Multiple fractures? How did it happen? What? He tripped on his dhoti? . . . That's sad. Do you know when mummy and daddy . . .? Yes, yes, I promise I'll visit him. No, I don't want to speak to Kala. I didn't call for her . . . No, we haven't fought. *(Quietly.)* Uncle, could you please tell me—what time did my parents leave the hospital? Good. Thank you. I promise to call Kala . . . and I promise to go to the hospital . . . Yes. I'll take Kala with me . . . No, I won't forget to take some payasam for him. Excuse me, I think the milk is boiling. Bye. *(Puts the phone down and crosses downstage towards the kitchen.)* Musicians! Sit down. They should be here any moment.

VISWAS. Where are you going?

LATA. I'm making coffee for all of us. *(Stops.)* I could make Bournvita for you, if you want. *(Notices Viswas observing the cupboard.)* Beautiful, isn't it? Solid rosewood. They don't make cupboards like these anymore.

VISWAS. What's inside?

LATA. Oh, more books. *(Viswas opens the cupboard.)* Be careful. Most of those books have turned yellow. The pages will crumble if you touch them.

VISWAS *(removes a splendid brocade shawl).* Oh, wow! Look at that!

LATA. Isn't it splendid?

VISWAS. I'm going to ask for this as dowry.

LATA. No. He won't give it to you.

VISWAS. Why not?

LATA. Same reason why he won't sell the house. It belonged to my grandfather.

VISWAS. Looks like I should be lucky if he parts with you.

LATA *(takes the shawl from Viswas)*. It was a present to granddad from the Mysore maharajah. He got this and an award from the maharajah during Dussehra.

VISWAS. What for?

LATA. Mummy did tell me once, but I've forgotten. She said this was his most prized possession. Every time he had visitors, he would quickly wrap this around, no matter how hot it was. He was the first among the educated elite class to shun western suits and wear kurtas and shawls like these on formal occasions. *(Putting the shawl back into the cupboard.)* Now sit down while I do my work.

VISWAS. Can I sit in the kitchen and watch you?

LATA. No, thanks. I'll get nervous.

VISWAS. When my mother comes here, she'll want to watch you make coffee. Be prepared.

LATA *(as she exits)*. First my parents have to watch you make a monkey of yourself. *(Exits.)*

VISWAS *(calling after her)*. She has eyes like a hawk, my mother! She'll even check to see how far up your legs are tanned so she'll know whether you wear mini skirts or not!

*Viswas wanders around. He looks at a bookshelf and removes a book halfway. He hesitates, and then puts it back and dusts his hands. He moves towards the old-fashioned phone, picks it up and puts the receiver to his ear. He is shocked to hear a phone ring. He quickly replaces the receiver.*

LATA *(off, calling out loudly).* Viswas, get that, please.

VISWAS *(looks around, confused).* What? Where? *(Realizes it is from the living room.)* Yes! Yes! I've got it. I'm getting it. *(Crosses to the living room, answers the phone.)* Hello? . . . That's the number. Yes, this is the residence of Jairaj Parekh . . . No, he's not in . . . Me? Who am I? I–I–I'm nobody. Just the . . . just the . . . butler. *(Puts on an atrocious south Indian accent.)* I'm butler, saar. Saar and amma going out. I taking message.

LATA *(enters).* Viswas, who is that?

VISWAS. When they coming? They not telling . . . One nimit. I asking missy amma. *(Comes to the hall.)* Someone for your father.

LATA. Who is it?

VISWAS. He didn't say. Why don't you speak to him?

LATA. I'm busy. Take his number and say father will call back as soon as he comes. Unless it's Muthiah. Tell him they've just come and gone and won't be back till tomorrow.

*Lata exits to the kitchen. Viswas goes to the living room.*

VISWAS *(on the phone).* Hello. Missy amma saying they coming soon. Yourself be kind and give name and message . . . Yes, Yes I writing down messages . . . What you're saying, saar? I know writing message. I'm graduate in English honours . . . Yes, yes. You tell, good name? . . . *(As if writing.)* . . . Chag-an-lal Chadani . . . Chaganlal Chadani, is it not? . . . See I told you. And message? . . . You want . . . to . . . buy . . . property—offer . . . of . . . ninety . . . still open. *(Reads.)* You want to buy property. Offer of ninety still open. Is it not? . . . See I told you. *(Suddenly dropping the accent.)* Wait a minute!

You're the one—you want to build a shopping complex, right? . . . Never mind who I am. I have a message for you from Mr Jairaj Parekh. He still hasn't changed his mind. He's not interested. I also have a message for you from his son-in-law-to-be. Call back after ten years. He may be interested in your offer. Good bye! *(Hangs up and returns to the hall.)*

LATA *(enters)*. Who was that?

VISWAS. No one. Some poor old chap seeking employment. He wanted to know if there was a vacancy for a butler.

LATA. A butler? Are those still around? *(Exits.)*

*Viswas makes to sit but stops. He looks at the cupboard, goes towards it and opens it. He looks to see if Lata is around. Satisfied she isn't, he removes the shawl and wears it and struts around.*

VISWAS. What a granddaddy she had! He must have been a terror. No wonder her father is a weirdo. *(Clears his throat and puts on a mock-father voice.)* So, you want to be a dancer. Hah! Hah! Hah! Son, you will never amount to anything in life. Look at me. Look at what I have achieved. Yes. Look. Look. Look. *(Points to the furniture.)* What's that you say? There's more to life than money? You ungrateful wretch!

*Unnoticed by him, Jairaj Parekh and Ratna Parekh enter. They stop and stare at his antics. They are both in their sixties, but very erect and energetic from years of rigorous training.*

VISWAS *(continues dramatically)*. Where will you go being a dancer? Nowhere! What will you get being a dancer? Nothing! People will point at you on the streets and laugh and ask, 'Who is he?' 'He is a dancer.' 'What does he do?' 'He is a dancer.' 'Yes, but what does he do?' 'He is a dan . . .' *(Notices them.)* Sir! *(Grins stupidly and shrugs embarrassedly.)* I got bored waiting . . . *(Jairaj and Ratna don't respond.)* I love dancing. Not disco or anything like that. You know, our dances. There's so much more in them. You know what I mean? *(Shouts.)* Lata!

JAIRAJ. Please put the shawl back.

VISWAS. Yes, yes . . . *(Folds it clumsily.)* . . . I'm sorry . . . it is a lovely shawl.

RATNA. Give it to me. *(Stretches out her hand.)*

*Viswas gives the shawl to her. She folds it neatly and puts it back into the cupboard. Jairaj is staring at Viswas. Ratna sits down.*

RATNA. Please sit. *(Viswas sits awkwardly. Without looking at Jairaj.)* Sit down.

JAIRAJ *(moves to sit, then stops abruptly and shouts).* Lata! *(Sits.)*

*Embarrassing silence.*

LATA *(enters).* I didn't hear you come in. I spoke to Muthu uncle and he said you'd already left. What took you so long? *(Silence.)* Anyway, I've made coffee for us and Bournvita for our guest. He hates instant coffee. Mummy, maybe you should make some filtered coffee for him some time. *(Now uneasy.)* I'll be back in a minute! I'm sorry if I interrupted the friendly conversation. *(Exits.)*

*The others stare at one another.*

RATNA *(bursts out).* This is terrible! What are we going to do?

JAIRAJ. There's no use worrying . . .

RATNA. This has never happened before! In all my life.

JAIRAJ. In all our lives . . .

RATNA. In all our lives, I can't remember ever being in such a crisis.

JAIRAJ. It's not a crisis.

RATNA. Crisis, problem, whatever!

JAIRAJ. We've had problems before.

RATNA. But never one like this. Oh God! What will we do?

JAIRAJ *(comforting her)*. We'll think of something. First, shut up.

*Ratna stops. Viswas has been staring at them dumbfounded.*

VISWAS. Look, I know I haven't made a very good first impression, but I would be more comfortable if you didn't think of me as a crisis or a problem.

RATNA. What are you talking about?

VISWAS *(at a loss for words, laughs nervously)*. Could I ask you the same question?

JAIRAJ. We were not talking about you. We don't even know you.

VISWAS. My name is Viswas and . . .

JAIRAJ *(irritated)*. We know that. But we don't know you well enough to think of you as a problem or anything. Understand?

VISWAS. That's a relief!

JAIRAJ. What? That we don't know you?

VISWAS. No. That you don't think of me as a problem.

RATNA. Ten days! That's all we have.

JAIRAJ. We'll find someone else.

RATNA. Who? Everyone's booked.

JAIRAJ. We could ask Seshadri. He knows our repertoire.

RATNA. Seshadri? Are you mad? He's rehearsing with Chandra Kala.

JAIRAJ. He'll only need a day's rehearsal.

RATNA. He won't have the time.

JAIRAJ. He won't be rehearsing with Chandra Kala all day for ten days.

RATNA. When he's not rehearsing with her, he is sleeping with her.

JAIRAJ. You don't know that for sure. You mustn't listen to gossip.

RATNA. It's not gossip. I have seen it with my own eyes.

JAIRAJ. When?

RATNA. When we were in Moscow, at the hotel. At three o'clock in the morning, I saw him sneak down the corridor and into her room.

JAIRAJ. What were you doing in the hotel corridor at three in the morning?

RATNA. Watching to see whose room you had sneaked into.

JAIRAJ. I was downstairs drinking vodka with the Yakshagana troupe.

RATNA. How do you know?

JAIRAJ. How do I know what?

RATNA. That was too quick an answer. How do you know which night I'm talking about?

JAIRAJ. There was only one night in Moscow I stayed up late drinking vodka . . .

RATNA. That was ten years ago. How can you remember so clearly?

JAIRAJ. If you can remember Seshadri sneaking down a hotel corridor ten years ago, I can remember getting drunk with a gang of Yakshagana men with plucked eyebrows and bad make-up.

VISWAS *(clears his throat)*. I know this is none of my business, but aren't you straying away from the problem? From what I gather, the problem is that you need someone desperately within ten days. Someone like this Seshadri, but not Seshadri because he is too busy doing whatever he is doing.

JAIRAJ. You are intelligent.

VISWAS *(overjoyed)*. Thank you.

RATNA. How does that help us?

JAIRAJ. You're right. It doesn't.

VISWAS. Maybe if I know what it is you want . . .

LATA *(enters with coffee and Bournvita)*. Sorry I took so long. The gas got over. I had to tilt the cylinder. *(To Viswas.)* I should have called you for help but I thought it may not be a good idea. *(To Ratna.)* So, what do you think of him?

RATNA. We aren't thinking of him.

LATA *(serving)*. Oh, then it's me you were thinking of. Viswas, I hope you haven't told them you don't have any money. *(To Ratna.)* Don't believe him. His father owns half the buildings on Commercial Street.

VISWAS. We haven't been discussing my money.

LATA. Oh, why not?

VISWAS. I seem to be in the middle of a problem.

LATA. Something you haven't told me? Is it financial?

VISWAS. No! What I mean is your parents seem to have a problem and I'm in the middle of it.

JAIRAJ. You are not. You don't even know what the problem is.

RATNA. Lata! You should be the one to worry.

LATA. What about?

RATNA. About Srinivas breaking his arm. Who will play the mridangam for your performance?

LATA. Oh my God! It didn't strike me. Of course, he broke his arm!

RATNA. Why did it have to be him? I wouldn't have minded if Muthiah had broken his neck.

JAIRAJ *(to Viswas)*. C.V. Srinivas, our mridangist.

RATNA. A flutist or violinist we can do without, but this . . .

JAIRAJ *(to Viswas)*. He tripped on his dhoti.

LATA. This is a crisis.

VISWAS. It's a special talent.

LATA. Of course it is. Playing any instrument requires a special . . .

VISWAS. I meant wearing a dhoti. You have to get the hang of it. I wore one once. You've got to kick it out of your way. Like a sari. Of course, I've never worn a sari, so I . . .

LATA. Viswas, do you mind? We are in the middle of a problem.

RATNA *(to Viswas)*. Sreenu has been wearing a dhoti ever since he grew out of half-pants. He must have been drunk.

VISWAS. You're right.

RATNA. The fool!

LATA. Viswas, please drink your Bournvita. This is serious.

*Jairaj offers Ratna coffee.*

RATNA *(waving her hand).* I don't want it. *(Rubs her forehead.)*

JAIRAJ. Worrying is not going to help. Think of all the people we know.

LATA. Have you asked Seshadri uncle?

RATNA. Certainly not!

LATA. Good. I hate that pot-bellied lech.

*Ratna gets up.*

JAIRAJ. Where are you going?

RATNA. To get an Aspro for my headache.

JAIRAJ. You are always taking Aspro. *(Follows Ratna.)* Don't take too much Aspro.

RATNA. I tried Novalgin. It doesn't help.

JAIRAJ. You're going to kill yourself. Stop taking those tablets.

RATNA. I have to! I can't take this tension.

JAIRAJ. What tension? There's plenty of time. You're worrying about nothing.

RATNA *(excitedly).* Nothing? Our daughter is giving a performance that will make her career and she is not going to have a mridangam playing for her. How do you expect her to give her best? How do you expect her to dance? What will we announce to the President of India? There will be no dance tonight? Tell all those foreign diplomats to go home? In my life I've had problems . . .

JAIRAJ. Now don't start . . .

RATNA. Problems which you know about but conveniently forget!

JAIRAJ. Ratna, no . . .

RATNA. I did not go through all that to see our daughter's career finish overnight!

JAIRAJ. It's not . . .

RATNA. Finished! Just like me. Yes, your father was right. Dance has brought us nowhere. It's his curse on us. Nothing seems worth it anymore. Oh, it is all so . . . worthless. You should have listened to your father. He was right. We were never anything great, never will be, and nor will our daughter be anything but an average human being.

JAIRAJ. Lata is not average!

RATNA. If she can't dance, what else can she be?

JAIRAJ. There were times when we didn't dance.

RATNA. And look where we are.

JAIRAJ. We are fine! At least I am.

RATNA. You! You are nothing but a spineless boy who couldn't leave his father's house for more than forty-eight hours.

JAIRAJ. Ratna! Don't . . .

RATNA. You stopped being a man for me the day you came back to this house . . .

JAIRAJ. For forty years you've been holding that against . . .

RATNA. You're right, I'm worrying about nothing, because nothing is what we are!

JAIRAJ *(quietly)*. You are going mad.

LATA *(goes towards Ratna)*. Mummy, whatever happens, I'm going to dance at the fest. For all those people and for you.

JAIRAJ. Will finding a musician make me a man?

LATA. Daddy.

*Ratna exits to the bedroom. Pause.*

VISWAS. Maybe I should leave.

LATA. Yes. Maybe you should.

VISWAS. I'll come back some other time. *(Makes to go to the door.)*

LATA. If you want to.

VISWAS *(to Jairaj)*. Goodnight, sir.

JAIRAJ. Wait. Don't go yet.

LATA. Daddy, we've embarrassed him enough.

JAIRAJ. Please stay for a while.

*Pause.*

VISWAS. All right.

JAIRAJ. Sit down. *(Viswas sits.)* Drink your Bournvita.

VISWAS. I don't want it. I hate it.

JAIRAJ. Take it away, Lata.

LATA *(picks up the tray)*. You haven't had your coffee.

JAIRAJ. I don't want it. I hate coffee. *(Lata looks at Jairaj.)* I always have. *(Lata exits. Jairaj looks at Viswas.)* I'm sorry. We are usually a little more hospitable to our guests than this. Please excuse us.

VISWAS. I understand.

JAIRAJ. Do you?

VISWAS. Yes.

JAIRAJ. What do you understand?

VISWAS. That you are worried about Lata's performance and so you couldn't really pay much attention to me.

JAIRAJ. It's not just the performance.

VISWAS. Then what is it?

*Pause.*

JAIRAJ. Do you drink?

VISWAS. Well. No. Yes. Sometimes with friends. But never in front of elders.

*Jairaj goes to the cupboard. As he is opening it, Lata enters. He quickly closes the cupboard.*

LATA *(to Viswas).* I'm sorry. This just seems to be the wrong day . . .

JAIRAJ. It's all right. I've finished apologizing to your friend.

LATA. Good. Then he can leave and come back some other time and . . .

JAIRAJ. Lata, go to your mother's room and sleep with her tonight.

LATA. She's in one of her moods. You know how she gets.

JAIRAJ. Yes, I know. That's why I'm sleeping in your room tonight.

LATA. But she'll tell me the miseries of her life. I don't want to hear that all night.

JAIRAJ. You'll only hear them. I've lived through them.

LATA. Oh! *(Mutters to herself.)* That's one thing I'll never do. Bore my children talking about the failures in my life! *(Exits to the bedroom.)*

*Jairaj goes to the cupboard, and removes a bottle of whisky and a glass. He pours.*

VISWAS. Not too much for me. Just a little . . .

JAIRAJ. Soda?

VISWAS. Well . . .

JAIRAJ. Good. We don't have any. Drink it neat. Don't ask for ice. I'm not going to get it for you. *(Gives Viswas the glass.)*

VISWAS. What about you?

JAIRAJ. Straight from the bottle. Cheers. *(They drink.)* I'm not supposed to be drinking.

VISWAS. Is that why you hide it in the cupboard?

JAIRAJ. Shut up and drink.

   *Viswas and Jairaj drink in silence.*

VISWAS. You were going to tell me what's worrying you.

JAIRAJ. Was I?

VISWAS. Yes. That's why you asked me to stay, I think.

JAIRAJ. Oh! It's not worrying that's worrying me.

VISWAS. No? Then what is it?

JAIRAJ *(to himself)*. Stopping. And looking back. And seeing that you haven't gone very far. And won't go much further.

VISWAS. Phew!

JAIRAJ. Tell me about your life.

VISWAS. My life? There's nothing much to tell. It hasn't started yet.

JAIRAJ. It hasn't started yet! You can wait till you are sixty for it to start and it won't. *(Drinks.)* So, your father is a paanwalla.

VISWAS. Mithaiwalla.

JAIRAJ. Makes a lot of money?

VISWAS. It's the family business. It's okay. My father has really made good money from his buildings.

JAIRAJ. Hmm. Black.

VISWAS. Jet black.

JAIRAJ. Buildings, is it?

VISWAS. Yes.

JAIRAJ. Strange.

VISWAS. What?

JAIRAJ. That's how my father made his money.

VISWAS. Buildings?

JAIRAJ. Houses, bungalows. Bought them real cheap. When the British left, there was a real demand for these bungalows. He made a lot of money. One of the richest men in town. Amritlal Parekh. The sethji of the city. Do you know what he did with all that? He spent it all in reconstructing India. Sounds very patriotic, doesn't it? All he did was give out a lot of personal loans to friends and relatives. Gullible—that's what he was—my father.

VISWAS. My father wouldn't loan money to me if I wanted it.

JAIRAJ *(laughs loudly)*. Neither did my father. He gave to everyone except me.

VISWAS. Why?

JAIRAJ *(drinks)*. The craft of a prostitute to show off her wares—what business did a man have learning such a craft? Of what use could it be to him? No use. So no man would want to learn such a craft. Hence anyone who learnt such a craft could not be a man. How could I argue against such logic?

VISWAS. But you fought back. That's good. You did what

you wanted to do. You were steadfast.

JAIRAJ *(sarcastically)*. Brave.

VISWAS. Yes, and brave too.

JAIRAJ. Words! Brave words. That's all.

VISWAS. What happened?

JAIRAJ. What happened? Nothing. *(Laughs.)* That was the trouble. Nothing happened. *(Laughs again.)* Didn't you hear my wife? Nothing is what we are! After forty years, she tells me she doesn't think of me as a man. Just a spineless boy. And you know what I think? I think she is right!

VISWAS. Why?

JAIRAJ. She knows why.

VISWAS. You must have hated your father.

JAIRAJ. Maybe.

VISWAS. Lata told me you respected him a lot.

JAIRAJ. Did she say that?

VISWAS. Yes. That's why you have kept this portion unaltered, almost like a shrine in memory of him.

JAIRAJ. Rubbish. This was my world. I have kept it the same because it's mine. This is where I spent my childhood. I removed his memories. The gardens. He had plenty of spare time. He used to do a lot of gardening. A rose garden. Creepers climbing the walls. When he died, I had everything removed. Pulled it all out from the roots. When Ratna and I made some money from our dance school and performances abroad, we extended the front of the house. We had a lot of visitors, you see. We did make a name abroad and that made us local celebrities.

VISWAS. And the shawl? Why have you kept his shawl? *(No*

*reply.)* It's a beautiful shawl. I asked Lata if you would give it to me as dowry. Just joking, you understand. I don't really want anything. She said you wouldn't part with it because it was your father's.

*Jairaj goes to the cupboard and removes the shawl. He gives it to Viswas.*

JAIRAJ. Let me see how you look wearing it.

*Viswas wraps it clumsily around himself.*

VISWAS. It's fantastic. It will go very well with a sherwani.

JAIRAJ. Do you like it?

VISWAS. Oh, yes!

JAIRAJ. You can have it then.

VISWAS. Oh! I don't know how to thank you. It's very generous of you. I promise to take good care of it. I'll fold it neatly and put it in a bag and . . .

JAIRAJ *(takes the shawl, folds it and places it on the sofa).* I didn't mean you can take it now. When you are married to Lata.

VISWAS. I'm sorry. I misunderstood. Yes, of course. *(Takes his hand and shakes it vigorously.)* Thank you, sir. Thank you very much!

JAIRAJ *(removes his hand from Viswas's clasp).* It's only a shawl. Most boys would ask for a Maruti van.

VISWAS. No, I wasn't thanking you for the shawl. Thank you for agreeing to our marriage. You approve of me!

JAIRAJ. I approve of you?

VISWAS. Yes.

JAIRAJ. And you approve of us?

VISWAS. Yes!

JAIRAJ. Good, then go home. And ask your father to call me some time.

VISWAS. Yes, sir. Certainly. *(Goes towards the living room doorway.)* One thing Lata was right about. You are different. *(Exits.)*

*Jairaj smiles slightly. He picks up Viswas's glass, finishes the drink and puts the glass back in the cupboard. He picks up the bottle, takes one last swig before closing it and putting it back. He looks at the shawl he is about to pick up.*

RATNA *(enters)*. Jairaj? Has he gone?

JAIRAJ. Yes. How are you feeling?

RATNA. Just awful.

JAIRAJ. Where's Lata?

RATNA. Fast asleep on our bed. Wonder why she did that?

JAIRAJ. Yes. Wonder why?

RATNA. Don't pretend. You asked her to console me, didn't you?

JAIRAJ. Are you consoled?

RATNA. It doesn't matter. You'll have to sleep in her room.

JAIRAJ. I'll manage. *(Hiccups.)*

RATNA *(sniffing)*. You have been drinking, haven't you?

JAIRAJ. A little. That boy wanted a drink very badly. I kept him company.

RATNA. I don't believe you. You have been drinking quite a lot. I can tell by just looking at you.

JAIRAJ. Maybe.

RATNA. And where did you get the liquor from? Lata makes sure there is none in the house at any time.

JAIRAJ. Now you are the one who is pretending.

RATNA. What do you mean?

JAIRAJ. You know I hide it in the cupboard.

RATNA. If I had known, I would have taken it away.

JAIRAJ. You did take it away. And you put it back. After diluting it with water.

RATNA. You are drunk.

JAIRAJ. Next time you want to drink, don't bother topping it with water. You have to drink more every time to get the same kick.

RATNA. I don't need to get a kick like you! I–I have a little bit now and then to settle my nerves.

JAIRAJ. Sit down.

RATNA. Why?

JAIRAJ *(making Ratna sit)*. Sit down, Ratna Devi . . . can I get you a drink? *(Goes to the cupboard.)*

RATNA. Please, Jai. I'm in no mood for jokes.

JAIRAJ. Jai? You called me Jai? *(Takes out the bottle and opens it.)* You haven't called me Jai in God knows how many years. This calls for a celebration. Here. *(Offers Ratna the bottle.)*

RATNA. I always use the glass.

JAIRAJ *(goes to the cupboard to get a glass)*. Good. We haven't expressed ourselves to each other so well for a long time. Maybe we should drink together more often. *(Pours.)* At least we will be more honest with each other.

RATNA *(takes the drink)*. When have I been dishonest with

you? *(Takes a large gulp.)*

JAIRAJ. See what I mean about diluting it? Some more? *(Ratna shakes her head.)* Feeling better? *(She nods.)* Good. Then we can talk.

RATNA. Yes. I have decided we could ask Chandra Kala to lend Seshadri, as a favour. She may need our help some day, so she is bound to oblige.

JAIRAJ. Good thinking.

RATNA. It's settled then. I'll call her in the morning. *(Makes to go.)*

JAIRAJ *(abruptly)*. Do you think we would have been happier if we hadn't come back?

RATNA *(confused)*. Are you talking about . . . ?

JAIRAJ. Yes.

RATNA. Why bring it up now after forty . . .

JAIRAJ. You brought it up. What did you say? I stopped being a man for you because we couldn't survive on our own . . .

RATNA. I didn't say it like that!

JAIRAJ. Your face tells me you did.

RATNA. You mustn't take notice of what I say when I'm upset.

JAIRAJ. That is the only time you make sense to me.

RATNA. I'm going to bed. I suggest you do the same.

JAIRAJ. What did you want me to do? Carry on staying at your uncle's . . .

RATNA. Don't!

JAIRAJ. Stay with him after what he said . . .

RATNA. Will you please . . . !

JAIRAJ. Is that what you wanted me to do?

RATNA. Don't say it!

JAIRAJ. Look the other way while your uncle . . .

RATNA. Please!

JAIRAJ. While your uncle asked you to go to bed with him? Would I have been a man then? Giving my wife to her own uncle because he was offering us food and shelter? Would you have preferred that? Do you think your uncle made such interesting proposals to all his nieces? No! That would be a great sin. But you were different. You were meant for entertainment. Of what kind was a minor detail. So what was wrong with going back to my father? At least my father didn't make . . .

RATNA (*screaming*). Stop it!

JAIRAJ (*quietly*). I'm sorry. You mustn't take notice of what I say when I'm drunk.

RATNA. Please forgive me. I didn't mean anything I said when I was upset . . .

JAIRAJ. You don't believe what you said was true?

RATNA. No.

JAIRAJ. Funny, I do.

RATNA. You know how anxious I am about Lata's performance. If she does well, she will be a national figure. Then if we butter up the right ministers, we can even get foreign tours arranged. You know how hard we had to struggle. I just want to make sure Lata won't have to face the same difficulties. You should understand how I feel . . .

JAIRAJ. Don't change the subject.

RATNA. I'm only explaining.

JAIRAJ. If that's how you felt about me, I must congratulate you for hiding it so well all these years. Don't feel bad about it. It was bound to spring up some time. You're only human.

RATNA. I'm human and so are you! So what if you couldn't support your family on your own? You were interested in . . . higher things. Something better than just working for money alone. And since your father had this house and could support us, there was no reason why we couldn't . . .

JAIRAJ. After leaving him? Coming back and accepting defeat?

RATNA. That was an impulsive decision—to leave. We were both to blame.

JAIRAJ. That is very kind of you. Not to blame me alone. Or maybe it's not kindness. Something deeper than that. Like . . . guilt? You forgive me and I forgive you. Forgive what you did to Shankar . . .

RATNA. Don't mention that name to me!

JAIRAJ. Oh, no! I won't. I forgive you. I will never mention Shankar again . . .

RATNA. Oh! *(Weakly.)* You promised. Oh, I only wish . . .

JAIRAJ. What? That we could start again?

RATNA. Oh, I don't know. It all seems so petty now.

JAIRAJ. Not worth the . . . sacrifices.

RATNA *(looks at Jairaj)*. It was too great a price to pay, Jai.

JAIRAJ. And yet you wish the same life for your daughter.

RATNA. Times have changed and things will be easier for her in some ways. Of course, she is talented and can become famous.

JAIRAJ. Will that make all we've been through worth something?

RATNA. Yes! I wish Lata more fame than we have had. Why, she can be the best! We just have to push her a bit and, with our experience behind her, she can't fail. Yes. I'll do anything to see that she reaches the top. Even if it means being sweet to that bitch Chandra Kala.

JAIRAJ. Good. You sound normal again.

RATNA. Within ten days, you'll see. Our Lata will be the talk of the town. I've taken care of the critics already. I've promised C.V. Suri I'll make him the chief guest at the Navratri festival. That old fogey loves to be garlanded on stage. And if he gives Lata a rave review, the others wouldn't dream of doing differently. Things would have been perfect if that Sreenu hadn't . . . Anyway, we'll think about that tomorrow. I'm going to sleep now. *(Makes to exit.)*

JAIRAJ *(puts back the bottle and glass into the cupboard)*. What do you think of Viswas?

RATNA *(stops)*. Who?

JAIRAJ. The boy Lata brought home tonight.

RATNA. He's all right. A bit strange. But okay. Why?

JAIRAJ. No particular reason. I've just agreed to them getting married, that's all.

RATNA. He's well off, isn't he?

JAIRAJ. From what he told me, yes.

RATNA. And he will let her dance?

JAIRAJ. Yes.

RATNA. In that case *(as she exits)* just make sure the wedding is after the Navratri festival . . . *(Exits to bedroom.)*

*Jairaj yawns and is also about to exit to the bedroom when he notices the shawl. He goes and picks it up and makes to put it into the cupboard, but changes his mind.*

JAIRAJ *(to himself).* Your last memory. Soon I'll be rid of you too. Then I won't see you wearing this shawl, walking about this room. *(Flute, followed by mridangam.)* I won't see you wearing this shawl. I won't see you walking about this room. *(Paces up and down while the lights dim.)* I won't see you wearing this shawl walking about this room. Walking about—wearing this shawl.

*Jairaj wears the shawl. He is immediately fixed in a spotlight. The music builds up until suddenly* jathis *or dance syllables being recited can be heard. The living room now changes into a lovely rose garden. Spotlight picks up a young man with his back to the audience, dancing. He wears dancing bells and a band around his waist. A young woman is sitting in front of him. The characters have all changed. Jairaj becomes the father, Amritlal Parekh. Viswas becomes Jairaj. Lata is now Ratna. Their ages remain the same as those of the previous characters they played. It is now the 1940s.*

AMRITLAL *(shouting).* Jai! *(No response.)* Jairaj!

*Full lights. Jairaj mimes, motioning to the musicians to stop. The music stops.*

JAIRAJ *(shouting).* What?

AMRITLAL. When I call for you, please show your face.

JAIRAJ *(comes to what is now the main living room, the bells around his ankles ringing as he walks).* What is it, Father? I'm in the middle of an item.

AMRITLAL. What? Still in the middle? You've been at it the whole day.

JAIRAJ. Not the whole day. We had a long lunch break.

AMRITLAL. And how long will it last?

JAIRAJ. I don't know. Ratna and I take turns. Guruji decides when to pack up. Could you tell me what you want, Father? Guruji doesn't like to be kept waiting.

AMRITLAL. I want this din to stop. I want Guruji out, that's what I want.

JAIRAJ. You'll just have put up with it for some more time.

RATNA *(comes out of the dance hall)*. Are you coming? Guruji is waiting. He wants you to do the *jathiswaram* with me again.

AMRITLAL. Tell him he is occupied for the time being.

RATNA. Jai?

JAIRAJ. In a minute, Ratna.

RATNA. You know what he is like when he gets annoyed. *(Exits. Mimes, talking to Guruji and musicians.)*

JAIRAJ. Now what is it?

AMRITLAL. I'm expecting some people and I want those musicians out before they arrive.

JAIRAJ. They will leave when your guests come, I assure you.

AMRITLAL. I want them out now.

JAIRAJ. I can't just ask them to leave!

AMRITLAL. Doesn't he have any other students, your guru?

JAIRAJ. He is the most sought-after guru in India.

AMRITLAL. Then why is he spending his entire day in my house?

JAIRAJ. I will not get into an argument with you on that. Now if you will excuse me, I have work to do. *(Makes to exit to the dance hall.)*

RATNA *(enters from the dance hall, to Jairaj)*. Since we've stopped, the musicians want coffee. *(As she exits to the kitchen, to Amritlal.)* Musicians! They look for any excuse to pretend to feel offended. I'll bring tea for you.

AMRITLAL. Don't bother about me. Look after your guests!

RATNA. The coffee won't take time. The decoction is ready. *(Exits to the kitchen.)*

JAIRAJ. I can't even have a decent rehearsal in this house.

AMRITLAL. You can't have a decent rehearsal in this house? I can't have some peace and quiet in my house! It's bad enough having had to convert the library into a practice hall for you.

JAIRAJ. Why did you do it if you didn't want to?

AMRITLAL. I thought it was just a fancy of yours. I would have made a cricket pitch for you on our lawn if you were interested in cricket. Well, most boys are interested in cricket, my son is interested in dance, I thought. I didn't realize this interest of yours would turn into an . . . obsession.

JAIRAJ. Didn't you have your obsessions?

AMRITLAL. If you mean my involvement in fighting for your freedom, yes, it was an obsession.

JAIRAJ. You had yours. Now allow me to have mine.

AMRITLAL. How can you even compare the two?

JAIRAJ. As far as I can see, I can.

AMRITLAL. As far as you can see! You can't see far, that is your trouble. Where is your dance going to lead you?

JAIRAJ. If we hadn't gained independence, where would your revolutions have led you?

AMRITLAL. I would like to see what kind of independence you gain with your antics.

JAIRAJ. The independence to do what I want.

AMRITLAL. I have always allowed you to do what you have

wanted to do. But there comes a time when you have to do what is expected of you. Why must you dance? It doesn't give you any income. Is it because of your wife? Is she forcing you to dance?

JAIRAJ. Nobody's forcing me.

AMRITLAL. She may be by influencing you. Maybe it's her, not you. That's one thing I regret. Consenting to your marriage.

JAIRAJ. Don't pretend. It suited your image—that of a liberal-minded person—to have a daughter-in-law from outside your community.

AMRITLAL. And for that I repent.

JAIRAJ. What do you mean?

AMRITLAL. Where does she go every Monday? *(Pause.)* You know and you don't tell me.

JAIRAJ. Where are your progressive ideas now?

AMRITLAL. This is different.

JAIRAJ. Where is the spirit of revolution? You didn't fight to gain independence. You fought for power in your hands. Why, you are just as conservative and prudish as the people who were ruling over us!

AMRITLAL. You are mistaken. Gaining independence was part of our goal. And someone has to be in charge. It's what we do now that counts. As you know, our priority is to eradicate certain unwanted and ugly practices which are a shame to our society.

JAIRAJ. Like dowry and untouchability.

AMRITLAL. That too. And . . . you know perfectly well what I mean.

JAIRAJ. You have no knowledge of the subject. You are ignorant.

AMRITLAL. We are building ashrams for these unfortunate women! Educating them, reforming them . . .

JAIRAJ. Reform! Don't talk about reform. If you really wanted any kind of reform in our society, you would let them practise their art.

AMRITLAL. Encourace open prostitution?

JAIRAJ. Send them back to their temples! Give them awards for preserving their art.

AMRITLAL. My son, you are the ignorant one. Most of them have given up their 'art' as you call it and have taken to selling their bodies.

JAIRAJ. I hold you responsible for that.

AMRITLAL. You have gone mad.

JAIRAJ. Give them their homes and give them their profession.

AMRITLAL. I will not have our temples turned into brothels!

JAIRAJ. And I will not have my art run down by a handful of stubborn narrow-minded individuals with fancy pretentious ideals.

AMRITLAL. Nobody is running down your art. It is the people who perform it and for what reason, that we are trying to . . .

JAIRAJ. All right then! You should be pleased that people from respectable families like yours are interested in reviving this dance. You should be encouraging us instead of being a hindrance.

AMRITLAL. I have no objection to your efforts in reviving the art, but I definitely do object to the people you are associating with.

JAIRAJ. Who do you mean?

AMRITLAL. Your guru. What kind of a family is he from?

JAIRAJ. His mother was not a devadasi, if that's what you wanted to know.

AMRITLAL. Why does he wear his hair so long?

JAIRAJ. Why do you ask?

AMRITLAL. I have never seen a man with long hair.

JAIRAJ. All sadhus have long hair.

AMRITLAL. I don't mean them. I meant normal men.

JAIRAJ. What are you trying to say?

AMRITLAL. All I'm saying is that normal men don't keep their hair so long.

JAIRAJ. Are you saying that he is not . . . *(Realizes the implication.)* Are you saying . . . ?

AMRITLAL. I've also noticed the way he walks.

JAIRAJ, *(angrily).* This is disgusting! You are insane!

RATNA *(enters with a tray and cups).* Coffee! Coffee for the artistes! Jai, do you want yours here or will you have it with Guruji? I'll get your father's tea in a minute. *(No reply from Jairaj.)* Jai? Shall I keep your coffee here or do you want to sit with Guruji? *(No reply.)* Well, I'll keep it here and I'll have mine . . .

JAIRAJ. Take it in, Ratna. I'll drink it with Guruji.

RATNA. It's all right. You can have it here. Keep your father company. I'll manage . . .

JAIRAJ *(roughly).* Give me the tray. I'll serve them. *(Takes the tray from Ratna.)* You can make tea for your father-in-law. *(Moves to the dance area.)*

RATNA *(stares after him uncomprehendingly, then to Amritlal.)* I'll make tea in a . . .

AMRITLAL. I don't want any tea.

RATNA. Really, it's no trouble . . .

AMRITLAL. Sit down. *(Quieter.)* Sit down, Ratna.

*Ratna sits. Jairaj mimes serving the musicians and talking to Guruji.*

RATNA. What happened?

AMRITLAL. Hmm?

RATNA. What happened between you two? He looked upset . . .

AMRITLAL. Nothing happened. We were just talking. I . . . mentioned something about long hair and . . . *(Ratna laughs.)* What's so funny?

RATNA. Oh, he told you?

AMRITLAL. What?

RATNA. That he is planning to grow his hair long? It would enhance his abhinaya.

AMRITLAL. I see. And was that his idea, or maybe yours?

RATNA. Actually, it was Guruji's suggestion.

AMRITLAL. Tell him that if he grows his hair even an inch longer, I will shave his head and throw him on the road.

RATNA *(a little frightened).* Yes. Now if you don't want tea, I'll go back to the class . . .

AMRITLAL. Where were you yesterday?

RATNA. I really must get back . . .

AMRITLAL. Where were you the whole of yesterday?

RATNA. I told you where I was going.

AMRITLAL. But where did you go instead?

RATNA. I don't know what you mean.

AMRITLAL. You had informed me that you were going to the Shiva temple.

RATNA. Yes. Like I do every Monday.

AMRITLAL. Every Monday, is it?

RATNA. Yes.

AMRITLAL. Times haven't changed. When we were newly married, Jai's mother and I were not allowed to go anywhere on our own, especially not to see the moving pictures. But we were allowed to go to the temple. So whenever we wanted to see the moving pictures, we would tell everyone at home that we were going to the temple. Nobody stopped us.

RATNA. If I wanted to see a film, I would tell you the truth.

AMRITLAL. That is because you know I won't object to your seeing a film.

RATNA. I would tell you anyway.

AMRITLAL. What if it wasn't a film you wanted to see? What if it were some place else where you know I wouldn't want you to go?

RATNA. Where would that be?

AMRITLAL. You know very well where, because that's where you go every Monday! *(Ratna does not respond.)* It was fortunate for me that it was Patel who saw you going there. I can trust him to keep his mouth shut. He called me, out of concern for our family name.

RATNA. I haven't done anything to spoil the family name.

AMRITLAL. But people assume the worst.

RATNA. Well, you can start by reforming such people instead of . . .

AMRITLAL. Don't preach to me! I know what I have to do.

RATNA. I have always been taught to speak to my elders with respect, but since I haven't done anything wrong there's no reason why I shouldn't speak up. Chenni amma is the oldest living exponent of the Mysore school and is the only link we have with the old school. She doesn't have a single student who is dedicated enough to absorb her knowledge. She is seventy-five and dying. There's nobody who even visits her, not even her relatives or her children. Oh, she does get the occasional journalist or a curious foreigner knocking at her door. But they don't do much for her, except maybe give her a few annas out of pity. But she doesn't mind all this. She doesn't mind at all being poor and lonely. What she is really frustrated about is that in her youth she did not have the freedom to express her art. All her childhood years were spent in training. Training which she could never use. All a waste— for her. She spends her time now at the temple steps, selling flowers. When she came to know that I was a dancer, she greeted me and pleaded, yes, pleaded with me to learn the art of abhinaya from her. She even tempted me by offering to teach me some old dance compositions which she knew by memory. It was important for her that she should impart her knowledge to someone worthy of it. And it was important for me to learn what she had to offer. So, instead of going to the temple every Monday, I go to her house.

AMRITLAL. And practise in her courtyard for all passers-by to see.

RATNA. Only those who are curious enough to peep over her wall to see where the sound of dancing bells are coming from.

AMRITLAL. Your bells. The sound of your bells.

RATNA. Yes.

AMRITLAL. The sound of your bells coming from the courtyard of a prostitute.

RATNA. She is seventy-five years old.

AMRITLAL. And people peer over her walls to see my daughter-in-law dancing in her courtyard.

RATNA. Yes. Dancing the divine dance of Shiva and Parvati.

AMRITLAL. And you feel what you are doing is right?

RATNA. Yes. My husband knows where I go and I have his permission.

AMRITLAL. Your husband happens to be my son. And you are both under my care. It is my permission that you should ask for.

RATNA. You would not have given it to me.

AMRITLAL. And I never will.

RATNA. If you don't allow me to visit her, then . . . then I'll have to ask her to come here!

AMRITLAL. Never. Not to this house, ever.

RATNA. What objection do you have to a withered old lady coming to your house? It is my dancing in her courtyard that you mind.

AMRITLAL. You will not. That is all. I need not give you any reason for it.

RATNA. You can't stop me from learning an art!

AMRITLAL. I don't want you seeing that woman again, that's final. And that is all I have to say. You may go. I'm sorry I've kept you from jingling your bells. My request is that you finish with your session as quickly as you can and see that your Guruji leaves before my visitors arrive. God forbid that they should bump into one another.

JAIRAJ *(enters with the tray)*. They've finished their coffee. Why didn't you serve them sweets? One of them hinted he wanted to eat sweets. You know how they love to feel insulted. *(To Amritlal.)* I have to pay the musicians.

RATNA. It's nice to know they are already feeling insulted. They can't feel any worse when we ask them to leave. Give me the tray.

JAIRAJ. I'll take it to the kitchen. He wants you to do a padam now. *(Looks at Amritlal.)* The older they get, the crankier they become. *(To Ratna.)* And who said anything about them leaving? *(To Amritlal.)* Four rupees. *(Exits to the kitchen.)*

AMRITLAL *(to Ratna)*. I'm leaving it to you. I'll give you ten minutes before I personally request them to leave.

RATNA. Don't worry. I'll think of an excuse.

AMRITLAL. Good. And if you promise me not to visit that woman again, I won't feel it necessary to restrict your movements. *(Ratna looks at him and laughs suddenly.)* What's so funny?

RATNA. I really feel sorry for you!

AMRITLAL. That's a strange way of showing that you feel sorry for me. Laughing like that.

RATNA. I really do feel sorry.

AMRITLAL. Why?

RATNA. Tomorrow, Jairaj starts learning another dance form—Kuchipudi.

AMRITLAL. So?

RATNA *(triumphantly)*. In Kuchipudi, the men dress up as women! *(Laughs triumphantly and exits to the dance hall.)*

*Ratna mimes, speaking to her guru. Jairaj enters and makes his way to the dance hall. He stops.*

JAIRAJ. Can I have the money now?

AMRITLAL. Yes, I'll give you the money now.

JAIRAJ. Four rupees.

AMRITLAL. Yes. You can pay them four rupees and tell them never to set foot in this house again.

*Pause.*

JAIRAJ. You can't do that!

AMRITLAL. I'm sorry, son.

JAIRAJ. But you promised.

AMRITLAL. Years ago.

JAIRAJ. You promised you would allow me to continue with my hobbies.

AMRITLAL. That was when you were a boy and dance was just a hobby. Grow up, Jairaj.

JAIRAJ. I don't want to grow up! You can't stop me from doing what I want.

AMRITLAL. As long as you are under my care . . .

*Ratna enters as if leading Guruji and the musicians to the door. She stands with folded hands near the door as they go out.*

JAIRAJ. Guruji! Why . . . (Watches them leave, then to Ratna.) Why did they leave? Did my father . . .?

RATNA. It's all right. They didn't feel offended. I told them we were tired and he said it was time he left. He will come back tomorrow.

AMRITLAL. He will not come here tomorrow. I will send him a personal letter of regret.

JAIRAJ (to Amritlal). As long as we are under your care . . . (Moves towards the bedroom.)

RATNA. Where are you . . . ?

JAIRAJ. As long as we are under his care! *(Exits.)*

RATNA. I won't bother asking you what happened.

*Amritlal goes to the old-fashioned phone and dials.*

AMRITLAL *(on the phone).* Hello? Patel? . . . Yes, I want a favour from you . . . The woman you saw my daughter-in-law with. Yes, that one. Could you send a doctor to see her? I believe she isn't well . . . Yes—and Patel? Please give her a donation of five hundred rupees on my behalf. I will send you a hundi . . . Please. I shall be very grateful to you . . . Thank you. *(Puts the phone down.)*

RATNA. That was very generous of you.

AMRITLAL. That was in compensation for depriving her of her only student.

*Jairaj enters with a bundle of clothes tied in a sari.*

JAIRAJ *(to Ratna).* Come on. I've packed some of your clothes. We're leaving.

RATNA. Where?

JAIRAJ. We'll decide that later. *(Gives Ratna the bundle.)* First, let's get out of here.

RATNA. But Jai, you haven't taken everything . . .

JAIRAJ. Never mind. *(Takes Ratna by the arm and leads her to the door.)*

RATNA. At least we could take all our belongings. We could leave tomorrow.

JAIRAJ. We don't need anything fancy. *(Turns around and speaks defiantly.)* As from now we are no longer under your care. And will never be again. Never. *(Exits, followed by a bewildered Ratna.)*

RATNA *(as she exits).* Jai! Jairaj!

*As soon as Ratna exits, the garden becomes the present-day living room. Amritlal becomes the older Jairaj as he removes the shawl. The older Ratna's voice from the bedroom picks up from where the younger one's trailed off.*

RATNA *(off).* Jairaj? *(Enters.)* Jairaj? Oh! You are still here? I didn't see you in Lata's room—I was wondering where you were. You haven't been drinking too much, I hope. Come to bed. I've asked Lata to go back to her room. She tosses and turns too much. It disturbs my sleep. And you can't share a blanket with her, she grabs it all for herself in her sleep. I pity that Viswas. *(Yawns.)* Come on. *(Jairaj slowly exits, followed by Ratna. Ratna's voice gradually trails off.)* You know, I don't think it is such a good idea asking Chandra Kala to lend Seshadri. They might plot to sabotage Lata's dance. He might give her the wrong tala. People can't make out whose mistake it is and they always blame the dancer. It happened once before when Nalini had taken Saraswati's cousin for her show . . .

*Lights fade out.*

## ACT II

*It is the 1940s. The younger Jairaj and Ratna are standing patiently while Amritlal censures them. There is a paper on the coffee table. It is two days after Jairaj and Ratna had left home. Evidently they have come back, defeated.*

AMRITLAL. All right. I will allow it. I realize, of course, that you have come back more out of necessity than any real intention of patching up what you have undone. I don't mind. It doesn't give me much pleasure to know that, but . . . I don't mind. And I don't gain much pleasure by reminding you that you had vowed never to come back to this house. No, I won't remind you of that. I am above it. But I definitely mind your silence. It carries too much hate. It never was my intention to get you to hate me. What parent would want that from his children? So I have changed my mind. I will allow you to dance. And I shall be very happy if you can earn your livelihood from it. If you ask me for money, I shall not refuse but I will be disappointed. I have been wise enough to invest my money in the right places. But don't think you have a right to all my wealth. I have far better things to do with it than hand it over to you. You may carry on using my library as your practice hall and your guru may come here twice a week in the mornings. I hope I have made myself clear. *(No response.)* Have I made myself clear?

JAIRAJ. Yes. Very clear. *(Moves to the stairs.)*

AMRITLAL. And Jairaj. *(Jairaj stops.)* Don't grow your hair any longer. *(Jairaj exits. To Ratna.)* And you need not learn from anyone else. You understand?

RATNA. You are very kind.

AMRITLAL. I want to see you both happy.

RATNA *(sarcastically)*. We are.

AMRITLAL. Are you?

RATNA. Can't you tell?

*Pause.*

AMRITLAL. Do you know where a man's happiness lies?

RATNA. No.

AMRITLAL. In being a man.

RATNA. That sounds profound. What does it mean?

AMRITLAL. Does Jairaj know where his happiness lies?

RATNA. He does. But I don't think it fits in with your idea of where it should be.

AMRITLAL. Yes. I am aware of that. And I am disappointed with that.

RATNA. Well, I'm sorry that you are disappointed. There is nothing much I can do about it.

*Pause.*

AMRITLAL. You can do a lot.

RATNA. I don't think I know what you mean.

AMRITLAL. I have seen the world. And I can recognize a clever woman when I see one.

RATNA. Thank you, I think.

AMRITLAL. How do you feel? How do you feel dancing with your husband? What do you think of him when you see him all dressed and . . . made up.

RATNA. You seem to forget. I married him because he is a dancer.

AMRITLAL. That's what he believes. I'm a little harder to convince.

RATNA. It's the truth.

AMRITLAL. Is it?

RATNA. Yes.

AMRITLAL. Or did you marry him because he would let you dance?

RATNA. That too.

AMRITLAL. More of that than the first?

RATNA *(a little ruffled)*. Well . . . yes.

AMRITLAL. Hmm. And you are intelligent enough to realize now that the decision to let you dance is in my hands, not his.

RATNA. You have made that very clear.

AMRITLAL. Don't worry. I have no intention of stopping you. I will let you dance.

RATNA. And Jairaj? You do want to prevent him from dancing, don't you? In spite of what you said.

AMRITLAL. A woman in a man's world may be considered as being progressive. But a man in a woman's world is pathetic.

RATNA. Maybe we aren't 'progressive' enough.

AMRITLAL. That isn't being progressive, that is . . . sick.

RATNA. Then why did you tell him just now that he could dance?

AMRITLAL. Tell me. How good is he as a dancer?

RATNA. He's good.

AMRITLAL. Good? Not brilliant? And you?

RATNA. Well, if I practise hard then . . .

AMRITLAL. Then you might become famous?

RATNA. I might.

AMRITLAL. Just as I thought. He is wasting his time. Poor boy.

RATNA. He isn't . . .

AMRITLAL. It's up to you now.

RATNA. What?

AMRITLAL. Help me make him an adult. Help me to help him grow up.

RATNA. How?

*Pause.*

AMRITLAL. It is hard for me to explain. I leave it to you. Help me and I'll never prevent you from dancing. I know it will take time but it must be done.

RATNA. I will try.

AMRITLAL. You'll have to do better than that.

RATNA *(more definite)*. All right.

*Moves towards the kitchen. Amritlal sits down. She stops and turns.*

And once he stops dancing—what will you do with him then?

AMRITLAL. Make him worthy of you.

*Ratna exits. Amritlal picks up the newspaper and becomes the older Jairaj. A telephone rings. The lights brighten. The garden changes into the living room, where the telephone is ringing.*

JAIRAJ. Ratna!

*The older Ratna enters from the kitchen.*

RATNA. Phone calls, phone calls, all morning! If it's that Muthiah again, I'll . . . I'll . . . *(Answers the phone.)* Hello.

Oh, hello, Dr Gowda. How nice of you to call. And thank you for the flowers. Lata was so pleased . . . Yes. Yes. Thank you. Oh—thank you! Yes, I'll tell her. She will be thrilled to hear that . . . Why, yes! Why shouldn't she be thrilled? Compliments like these from you—I don't mean because you are a minister or anything like that, but you are so knowledgeable about dance and also known to be so critical . . . If people like you praise her, then she has every reason to be thrilled. And if a person no less than the President of India gave her a standing ovation . . . Of course! As soon as Lata finished her tillana, he stood up and applauded . . .

JAIRAJ *(looks up from his paper)*. He was in a hurry to go to the toilet.

RATNA *(waves to him to shut up)*. Anyway, I really do appreciate you taking the trouble to call, especially since you are busy organizing the Indian festival in Canada. I can wake Lata up, but she is too tired. And after last night's performance she deserves a rest. Still, if you wish I could call her . . . Then I'll ask her to call you back? No. No. It's no trouble. I'll ask her to call you back . . .

JAIRAJ. Especially since you're busy organizing the Indian festival in Canada.

RATNA. And if you want any help from us in organizing, please do not hesitate to ask us. Jairaj and I will be pleased. After all, we've known you for so many years now, we are like a family . . .

JAIRAJ *(impatiently)*. You're overdoing it . . .

RATNA *(waves for him to keep quiet)*. By the by, have you decided on your selection committee? You must have more dancers this time. Not like the France fiasco. *(Laughs.)* Oh, you have? Anyone we know? Who? . . . *(Shocked.)* Who? . . . Chandra Kala? *(Quickly.)* Yes. Yes, of course. A very good dancer—twenty years ago. Of course I'm happy for her daughter Mala . . .

JAIRAJ. Oh no!

RATNA. Well, it helps to have your mother on the selection committee. Oh, I don't mean that Chandra Kala Devi would be partial. There is such a thing as ethics . . .

JAIRAJ. Is there?

RATNA. But you will have the final say, won't you? Oh, that's good . . . Oh, I am sorry. Of course, I didn't realize I was keeping you from important work. Thank you so much. Aye. *(Replaces the phone.)*

JAIRAJ. Don't push. You make yourself obvious.

RATNA. I'm not pushing. He called. *(Goes towards the bedroom.)*

JAIRAJ. Exactly. If he called, then he liked her. There's no need for you to force . . .

RATNA *(calling out)*. Lata! *(To Jairaj.)* Rubbish. Within the next few hours he'll forget about her. What with that Chandra Kala after him . . .

JAIRAJ. How do you know she's after him?

RATNA. He's put her on the selection committee! *(Calls out.)* Lata! Are you awake? *(To Jairaj.)* You say I'm pushing myself by talking to him, Chandra Kala is probably sitting on his lap!

JAIRAJ. She couldn't.

RATNA. Hmpf! That's what you think?

JAIRAJ. She's far too fat and he's far too skinny.

RATNA *(calling out)*. Lata!

LATA *(off)*. Yes, mummy, I'm awake! Give me five minutes.

JAIRAJ. Doesn't she want to read her review?

RATNA. She's afraid it's going to be bad.

JAIRAJ. But it's a rave review. Didn't you tell her?

RATNA. I thought I would surprise her. Let her come down. Do you want more coffee?

JAIRAJ. All right. Not too sweet.

RATNA. Then afterwards you can go to the news stall and buy the *Herald* and the *Times*.

JAIRAJ. Only the *Express* gives reviews the very next day. The others take at least another day.

RATNA. Not this time. They all promised. I promised C.V. Suri I would make him the chief guest at Navratri Utsav . . . *(Exits to the kitchen.)*

JAIRAJ *(shouting to Ratna)*. They have to give it in the same night. Most of them don't have the time. Unless they write the review before the performance, which sometimes they do. *(The phone rings.)* Ratna!

RATNA *(enters and goes towards the phone)*. Yes. Yes. Sit there reading a newspaper while the whole world is knocking at our door. *(Answers the phone.)* Hello . . . *(Sweetly.)* Oh hello, Seshadri. Did you sleep well? Yes, we read the *Express*. That C.V. Suri is such an intelligent critic, he really knows his subject . . . For what, Sesha? No, really. I don't know why you are apologizing . . . No. No! Sesha . . . it is really nothing. So what if you gave her the wrong tala in the beginning? I immediately stopped you, didn't I? Anyway, don't worry. It happens to the best of people. How is Chandra Kala? Please congratulate her on my behalf . . . Oh, you don't know? I thought she might have told you . . . Devaraj Gowda has put her on the selection team to choose dancers for Canada. I am so happy for her—and Mala. Well, I'll tell you a secret.

Devaraj called me and asked me if I wanted to be on the committee. Since I know almost all the dancers personally, it would be a very delicate situation for me to choose—but I told him that he mustn't waste any time in asking Chandra Kala. She is just the person, I told him . . . Oh, it is nothing! After all, what are friends for? . . . What? Yes. Yes. Certainly . . . Don't worry. I will see that you get in . . . Don't worry, Sesha. Within this year you will be in Canada . . . Yes. Yes. You must excuse me now, I think the milk is boiling. Thank you for calling. So kind of you . . . Yes. I'll tell her. *(Replaces the phone.)* One of these days I'm going to break his mridangam on his head! *(Moves towards the kitchen.)* Will idlis do or shall I make dosas for breakfast? *(Exits without waiting for an answer.)*

*Jairaj folds his paper and puts it down. Viswas enters, looking very excited. He has two papers with him.*

VISWAS. Did you read them? *Herald* and *Times*! Rave reviews!

JAIRAJ. Did you read *Express*?

VISWAS. No. Let me see it!

*He takes the* Express *eagerly and Jairaj takes the* Herald *and the* Times *as eagerly. They both simultaneously turn the pages.*

JAIRAJ *(reading.)* 'Lata Parekh—star of the festival.'

VISWAS *(reading.)* 'Lata excels!' Wow!

JAIRAJ *(flicks through the other paper)*. 'Lata leaves rest behind!' Wait till she reads this!

*Viswas reads while Jairaj goes towards the bedroom and calls out to Lata.*

JAIRAJ *(calling out)*. Lata! Come and read your rave reviews!

LATA *(off)*. I'm coming!

JAIRAJ. Viswas is here.

LATA *(off)*. Oh, in that case, give me two minutes.

VISWAS *(reading)*. 'Blessed with a supple figure and expressive face, Lata Parekh executed the adavus neatly and with precision . . .'

JAIRAJ *(calls into the kitchen)*. Viswas is here.

RATNA *(off)*. I'll make another cup. Ask him whether he has had breakfast.

VISWAS *(reading)*. 'Her nritya and abhitiaya were unparalleled and truly remarkable in a dancer so young in years. Under the expert guidance of her parents Smt Ratna and Sri Jairaj Parekh, she has blossomed into a superlative dancer. This is one star which will shine bright in the sky of Bharatanatyam.'

JAIRAJ *(reading)*. 'Her angashuddha and grip over rhythm stand head and shoulders above the rest, even surpassing veterans like Chandra Kala Devi. Truly, Lata Parekh, with perseverance and dedication will find her place amongst legendary artistes like Balasaraswati and Rukmini Devi.'

VISWAS. That's great. That's really . . . I don't know what angashuddha and all that means, but it sounds simply wonderful.

JAIRAJ. She's a genius! That's what it means. Our daughter is a genius.

VISWAS. 'A shining star in the sky of Bharatanatyam!'

JAIRAJ. These critics get carried away now and then.

VISWAS. Who cares? They liked her. They adored her!

RATNA *(enters with coffee)*. You see! Haven't all the critics . . .

*Lata enters. Immediately both men stand up and applaud.*

JAIRAJ. 'The discovery of the decade!'

VISWAS. 'A shining star!'

*Lata makes a mock namaste. Ratna places the tray on the table with a forced smile.*

LATA. Thank you. Thank you, one and all.

RATNA *(with a catch in her voice)*. Congratulations, Lata. *(They embrace.)* Now, sit down and drink your coffee.

JAIRAJ. And read your reviews! *(Gives Lata the papers.)* Here. Here and here.

*Lata and Jairaj sit.*

RATNA. Viswas, I hope you are staying for breakfast.

VISWAS. Oh, no, thanks. I've had mine already.

RATNA. It's only idlis. You can eat one or two.

*Viswas laughs uncomfortably. Ratna exits to the kitchen.*

*Viswas sits.*

LATA *(still reading)*. I can't believe it!

JAIRAJ. You'd better. You are famous now.

LATA. Mostly mummy's efforts. Pushing me forward.

JAIRAJ. I wouldn't give her the credit entirely.

LATA *(reading and laughing)*. This one actually liked my tillana. 'Her sculpturesque poses and flourishes were truly delightful to view'—that's a laugh.

JAIRAJ. They were very good. Even though you made them all up.

LATA *(giggles)*. I forgot the last jathi and simply posed till the music finished and I finished with a flourish.

VISWAS. But I liked those poses. They did remind me of sculptures like . . . you know, the one you see on post cards where the dancer is talking to a parrot or something.

JAIRAJ. In the tillana she wasn't supposed to be talking to a parrot.

VISWAS. Anyway, it looked good.

JAIRAJ. How can it look good? She had no business talking to a parrot in the middle of a tillana.

VISWAS. Ah, but we didn't know that. And I liked the way she finished with a flourish. We knew then it was time to clap.

JAIRAJ *(coldly)*. Drink your coffee.

LATA *(reading and laughing loudly)*. This one is hysterical. 'Her rendition of the ashtapadi from *Geeta Govindam* was tenderly intense and intensely tender. The audience was transported to Gokulam and witnessed Radha pining for the divine lover, who has failed to arrive. Lata's tearful expression and heaving bosom conveyed all that was humanly possible.' *(Laughing. To Viswas.)* My bosom was heaving because I was breathless from the varnam.

VISWAS. I didn't quite like that one.

JAIRAJ. You didn't like Jayadev's *Geeta Govindam*?

VISWAS. Oh no!

JAIRAJ. No?

VISWAS. Oh no! No! I mean, I don't have anything against him.

JAIRAJ. Then what was it you didn't like?

VISWAS. Well, nothing . . . Well, on second thoughts, I quite liked it.

JAIRAJ *(to Lata)*. Your friend didn't like the ashtapadi. Ask him what was wrong with it.

LATA *(still reading)*. Huh?

VISWAS. I didn't say I didn't like the ashtapadi.

JAIRAJ. You did.

VISWAS. No, I didn't.

JAIRAJ. Oh, you mean I'm hearing things. I'm growing old. Is that what you want to say?

VISWAS. No! I loved the ashtapadi. How can I hate something when I don't even know what it means.

LATA. But you can love it, I notice.

VISWAS. Well, it was tenderly intense and intensely tender and all that. But . . .

JAIRAJ. But what? You didn't like her interpretation? What did you want her to do? Talk to her parrot while she is waiting?

VISWAS. No, I didn't mean that.

LATA. Vishy, you're being wishy-washy again.

JAIRAJ. Speak up, son.

LATA. What was it that you didn't like?

VISWAS. It was too erotic.

*Silence.*

JAIRAJ. My wife danced that same item thirty years ago.

VISWAS. I admire her courage.

LATA. So—you feel it shouldn't be done?

VISWAS *(uncomfortably)*. I really can't say. I don't know much about these things.

JAIRAJ. But you think you know enough to pass judgement.

VISWAS. I'm not passing judgement. I simply gave my opinion, that's all.

JAIRAJ. I'm glad you have an opinion. You are welcome to it for whatever it is worth.

VISWAS. Look, I know I'm not very knowledgeable on the subject. I merely said that because it was Lata who was dancing and . . .

JAIRAJ. Finish what you were saying. *(Viswas remains silent.)* So now we are getting closer to your opinions. You don't want Lata dancing erotic numbers.

LATA. Daddy, you make it sound so crude. 'Erotic numbers'?

JAIRAJ. There's nothing crude about it. I danced the same item. For the army. A friend of ours arranged a programme and the money was good. Your mother was too scared and they only wanted a woman. So I wore your mother's costume, a wig and . . . whatever else was necessary to make me look like a woman, and danced. They loved it. They loved it even more when they found out I was a man. Of course, knowing the army, that may not be very surprising. *(To Viswas.)* What do you say about that?

VISWAS. I admire your courage. Look, I don't mean I object to her dancing. It is her passion and it wouldn't be fair for me to . . . All I'm saying is that . . . What am I saying? *(Thinks.)* Yes! That it really isn't necessary to make it so . . . you know. At least I don't think so. Of course, you may think so, but I don't. And I don't know what she thinks about it so . . . *(Shrugs his shoulders and laughs nervously.)*

LATA. It was choreographed by daddy thirty years ago for mummy. They won critical acclaim abroad for pieces like the ashtapadi. I fail to see why I can't perform the same piece today.

VISWAS. Yes. Of course. If that's what you really want. Nobody's stopping you.

JAIRAJ. Lucky for her. In the old days . . .

LATA *(to Viswas)*. Do you want to stop me? You can't. But do you want to?

*Pause.*

VISWAS. Do you remember what you told me? In this very room? One right away, and another let us see?

LATA *(smiling)*. Yes.

VISWAS *(sincerely)*. Does that still hold good?

LATA *(returning his sincerity)*. Yes.

VISWAS. Thank you. I hope your father will teach you some more . . . ashtapadis. *(To Jairaj.)* Now if you don't mind, I have to rush to the shop and supervise the making of jalebis. My father is busy chasing government officials to sanction a plan for a multi-storeyed mithai complex.

JAIRAJ. That would be a paradise for the Marwari community.

LATA. Won't you stay for breakfast?

VISWAS. No. I really must go before the cooks steal all the ghee. I'll just make my excuses to your mother and be on my way. *(Exits to the kitchen.)*

LATA. What do you think of him?

JAIRAJ. A bit strange, isn't he?

LATA *(sighs)*. He has his quirks. Like the rest of us.

JAIRAJ. Wonder what his father is like.

LATA. You'll soon meet him. *(Collects all the newspapers.)*

VISWAS *(enters and speaks hesitantly)*. I think you'd better see how your mother is feeling.

*Lata and Jairaj get up.*

LATA. What's wrong?

*Mahesh Dattani*

VISWAS. She is sitting there in the kitchen and crying.

LATA. Mummy! *(Exits to the kitchen in a hurry.)*

 *Jairaj slowly sits down.*

VISWAS. Mind you, she could have been cutting onions. I didn't notice.

JAIRAJ *(to himself)*. She will be all right. She is crying.

VISWAS. If you need me I could stay. *(No response.)* But I should really be going. So—if you don't mind, bye. *(No response. Shrugs his shoulders and mutters.)* Strange people. *(Exits through the living room.)*

 *Lata enters with Ratna.*

RATNA. It's all right.

LATA. Why don't you go up and lie down for a while?

RATNA. No, no. I'm okay.

LATA. Sit down. Shall I make you some coffee?

RATNA *(sits)*. No, just put the cooker on the stove.

 *Lata picks up the tray of coffee.*

JAIRAJ. Breakfast isn't ready? What were you doing in the kitchen? *(Lata looks at Jairaj disapprovingly and exits to the kitchen with the tray.)* One of your headaches? Or is it depression now that all the excitement of Lata's performance is over? It's too early in the day to drink.

RATNA. I don't want a drink.

JAIRAJ. Then any particular reason for this change in mood?

RATNA. Don't you have changes in moods?

JAIRAJ. Yes, but I don't sit in the kitchen crying.

RATNA. No. You sit in this room drinking!

JAIRAJ. I strongly recommend it. It keeps you from crying. Look at me. I never cry.

RATNA. That is because you are a . . . man!

JAIRAJ. Thank you. You haven't been so complimentary on previous occasions.

RATNA. Now don't start . . .

JAIRAJ. All right. We won't discuss my gender. Let's talk about you.

RATNA. Same thing. You talk about me, we talk about you.

JAIRAJ. Not if I choose the subject.

RATNA. When were we ever short of subjects?

JAIRAJ. A suitable subject. You are sixty and I'm sixty-two. It's time we become selective.

RATNA. What subject?

JAIRAJ. Shankar.

*Pause.*

RATNA *(pleading).* Anything but that. Please!

JAIRAJ. Oh, that displeases you immensely, doesn't it?

RATNA. Go on! Say it. Do your worst. I'm too tired to fight it.

JAIRAJ. No. That would be too easy. Let's talk about something else.

RATNA. You never talk, you attack!

JAIRAJ. That I learnt from you. Let's talk about Lata.

RATNA. What about her?

JAIRAJ. She is a dancer.

RATNA. Of course. Everyone has recognized that now. After my efforts . . .

JAIRAJ. Our efforts.

RATNA. Yes.

JAIRAJ. And you are happy?

RATNA. What a question to ask!

JAIRAJ. Are you happy for her?

RATNA. Of course! She . . . she is on her way to fame which is what I wanted for her. She had my blessings and guidance and now that her performance has been noticed by the right people, it shouldn't be very difficult for her to . . . Naturally, she will have to practise very hard and take her career very seriously. And then there's the foreign festival. I shall try my level best to see that she is included. I will use all my contacts and see that she is in. Yes, I have every reason to feel happy.

JAIRAJ. Have you read the reviews?

RATNA. Not all of them. Not yet.

JAIRAJ. Don't you want to read them?

RATNA. Yes! I was meaning to . . .

JAIRAJ. Why didn't you read them earlier?

RATNA *(picks up the papers)*. Well, I'll read them now. I was busy earlier what with Viswas dropping in and . . .

JAIRAJ. He brought the papers.

RATNA *(searches the papers nervously)*. Yes, but I was in the kitchen . . .

JAIRAJ. Weren't you interested in knowing what kind of reviews . . . ?

RATNA. I know what kind of reviews she's got . . .

JAIRAJ. You haven't even looked . . .

RATNA *(shouting)*. I heard. Rave reviews! The star of the festival! The dancer of the decade! And why shouldn't she get reviews like these? I deserved it. Spending sleepless nights arranging things. Sweet-talking the critics. My hard work has paid off, hasn't it? Hasn't it? *(Takes the papers and makes for the bedroom.)*

JAIRAJ. Where are you going?

RATNA. I have to paste these reviews in our album.

JAIRAJ. Our album?

RATNA. Yes.

JAIRAJ. You're going to paste her reviews in our album?

RATNA. Why not? There's plenty of space!

JAIRAJ. She deserves an album of her own.

RATNA. We don't have another album in the house.

JAIRAJ. Well, it's time we did!

RATNA. All right. You go and buy one. But these I'm pasting in my album.

JAIRAJ. Our album.

RATNA. Yes!

JAIRAJ. You are not pasting these reviews in our album.

RATNA. I will.

JAIRAJ. They don't belong there. *(Silence.)* Those critics gave her good reviews because she deserved them. They weren't doing you any favours. Face it, woman.

LATA *(off, cheerfully)*. Breakfast is ready. Come and get it!

JAIRAJ. I'm sorry, Ratna. I don't want to see you pasting those reviews in our album—pretending they are yours.

LATA (*off*). I'm serving hot, hot idlis! Eat them while they're hot!

JAIRAJ. Come. Let's have breakfast.

RATNA (*weakly*). I'm not hungry. (*Goes towards the bedroom, clutching the papers to her heart.*)

JAIRAJ. Ratna. (*Ratna stops.*) At least you have a daughter to be jealous of.

RATNA (*breaks down*). Oh! (*Exits quickly to her bedroom.*)

*Flute music takes over. Jairaj exits to the kitchen. The living room changes to the garden, bathed in moonlight. After a while the younger Ratna and Jairaj enter from the garden. Ratna is wearing a splendid Bharatanatyam costume which she has covered with a shawl. Jairaj is in an ordinary kurta-pyjama suit. He is evidently drunk.*

JAIRAJ. Walk in! The doors of hell are wide open.

RATNA. Shh!

JAIRAJ. Come in, Ratna Devi. Into the house of Sri Amritlal Parekh.

RATNA. Quiet. You'll wake . . .

JAIRAJ. The seth of the house is not in! He's away receiving awards for serving the nation—while his Lakshmi-of-the-house has been away receiving (*claps*) acclaim for her . . . talents.

RATNA. Shut up, Jai. You'll wake the baby.

JAIRAJ (*mockingly*). Oh! The baby! I forgot about him. Our little baby is fast asleep. We mustn't disturb him. Where are you going?

RATNA. Up. To see if he's all right.

JAIRAJ. Yes. Let's go up. Up. To see if baby's all right.

RATNA. You stay right here. Till you learn to be quiet.

JAIRAJ. Oh, I will be quiet! *(Whispers.)* Real quiet. Come, let's go up real quiet. *(Hiccups loudly.)*

RATNA *(pushes him away)*. Stay here, you drunkard. Don't you dare come up. *(Exits to the bedroom.)*

JAIRAJ *(to himself)*. Yes. Yes, I'll stay here. You go and see how our little Shankar is sleeping. Make sure his nose is dry and his bed isn't wet. His grandfather checks his mattress every morning. He even turns him over and checks his backside. Then grandfather sticks his finger in his mouth and checks his gums. Once his teeth are fully grown, I hope he bites him. *(Makes a snapping motion.)* Then when he grows up, I'll teach him how to dance—the dance of Shiva. The dance of a man. And when he is ready, I'll bring him to his grandfather and make him dance on his head—the tandava nritya. *(Strikes the Nataraja pose and hops about wildly.)* The lord of dance, beating his drum and trampling on the demon. *(Loses his balance and crashes. Ratna enters and helps him to his feet.)* How is our little lord of dance?

RATNA. I don't know. I was too scared to wake him so I didn't turn on the lamp. I just stood there by him but he didn't make a sound.

JAIRAJ. Good. Very good. He is in dreamland. Let him stay there. It's a far better place than this! Tomorrow I'm going to have a board hung outside this house saying, 'If ever there is a paradise, it isn't this, it isn't this, it isn't this . . .'

RATNA. Where is that new ayah? Probably fast asleep on the kitchen floor. She should have been near the baby, in case he gets hungry.

JAIRAJ. You should have been near the baby.

RATNA. I should have asked you to stay back. At least you would have been of some use here!

JAIRAJ. You didn't think I was useful there? I clapped the loudest. *(Claps loudly.)*

RATNA. Stop it. I'm going to bed. You can sleep here.

JAIRAJ. Oh. Have I disappointed you? You don't want to sleep with me? Never again?

RATNA. Don't talk nonsense. You are in no condition to be sleeping next to my baby. You stink.

JAIRAJ. And our baby can sleep next to you—with your strong smell of jasmine and cheap attar?

RATNA *(removes her shawl and throws it at Jairaj)*. Here, don't bother coming up.

JAIRAJ *(admiring Ratna's costume)*. What a beauty you are! Is that why you like to dance? To have men admire your assets?

RATNA *(scornfully)*. Why do you dance?

JAIRAJ *(mocking)*. Oh, but I don't. I'm not good enough.

RATNA. How can you be when you're drunk half the time?

JAIRAJ. Oh. I thought I drank because I wasn't good enough. Like the riddle—which came first: the egg or the chicken?

RATNA. You can riddle all you want. I'm tired.

JAIRAJ. Wait. I want to talk.

RATNA. What about?

JAIRAJ. Anything. I just want to talk to somebody. Even you.

RATNA. I'm tired.

JAIRAJ. The choice is between you and the ayah sleeping on the kitchen floor. I choose you.

RATNA. I choose to go to bed. *(Goes towards the bedroom.)*

JAIRAJ. Good idea. *(Also goes towards the bedroom.)*

RATNA *(turns around)*. What do you want from me?

JAIRAJ. The decency to talk to me when I'm lonely.

RATNA. Talk about what? Talk about how you insult me in front of other people? How you make me feel ashamed of you? How . . . how disgusting you are? Oh, for God's sake, Jairaj, do something useful before it's too late!

JAIRAJ. Do something that's useful to you, you mean.

RATNA. Do something. Do anything, but stop this mockery.

JAIRAJ. Do anything except be a dancer. Do something useful like choreographing items for you, or playing the flute.

RATNA. You are not even good at that anymore.

JAIRAJ. Whose fault is that?

RATNA. You go on drowning yourself in country liquor and ask me whose fault is that?

JAIRAJ. Whose fault is it that only you get invitations to dance?

RATNA. Surely not mine.

JAIRAJ. For one full year. For one full year I refused to dance— turning down offers because I didn't want to dance alone.

RATNA. I didn't ask for such a sacrifice. Tell me what you want in return. I'll do anything except sacrifice a year of my life in return.

JAIRAJ. I want you to give me back my self-esteem!

RATNA. When did I ever take it?

JAIRAJ. Bit by bit. You took it when you insisted on top billing in all our programmes. You took it when you made me dance my weakest items. You took it when you arranged the lighting so that I was literally dancing in your shadow. And when you called me names in front of other people. Names I feel ashamed to repeat even in private. And you call me disgusting.

RATNA. You just don't want to face it. It is me they want to see dancing.

JAIRAJ. A young beautiful woman, yes.

RATNA. A young beautiful woman! And you are jealous of me for that? What kind of a man are you?

JAIRAJ. Oh, you are so clever. No wonder you get along well with him.

RATNA. Get along well with whom?

JAIRAJ. My father. It was him, wasn't it?

RATNA. I don't know what you . . .

JAIRAJ. Don't pretend, I am not blind. Why did he allow us to dance? He knew he had us in his hands when we came back to him. We would have listened to anything he said.

RATNA. You would have listened. Not me. Yes! He realized he couldn't stop me. But he could stop you—through me.

JAIRAJ. You mean he would sooner watch me turn into a drunkard than see me dance?

RATNA. That is your own doing. He regrets it happened this way—and so do I.

JAIRAJ. Do you? I think you prefer it this way. He lets you do what you want and you have me out of your way. He in turn is grateful to you. My father is always asking me to grow up. Well, this is a perverse way of thrusting me into adulthood.

RATNA. To each his own perversity.

JAIRAJ. And what is yours?

RATNA. Agreeing with your father. Letting you off so that he could shape you into whatever shape he thinks a man should have. I should have guessed the result. When I say I regret it, I really mean that, Jai.

JAIRAJ. Oh, you are brilliant! I truly am jealous of you. You are quite a looker, quite a dancer and quite an actress! One has to hand it to you. You really have style. Not to mention brains. You destroy me first, then give the impression that there wasn't much to destroy in the first place, then blame it all on my father, then suggest I make myself useful by being your stage prop, then use words like 'regret' and expect me to shrug my shoulders, resign myself and believe that my calling in life is to serve you. Thank you very much for the talk. It has been an illuminating one. Good night. It's time to feed the baby. *(Lies down on the sofa and covers himself with the shawl.)*

RATNA. Oh, how easily you fool yourself. You think you are covered, don't you? *(Throws the shawl away from Jairaj.)* I'm not going to let you off so easily. You can't blame us for your state and get away with it. What do you want? Ask yourself? Do you want freedom? You had it and you came back to your prison. *(He covers himself again.)* Do you want to dance? *(Removes the shawl. He shuts his eyes and pretends to be asleep.)* Why didn't you accept those invitations when they came? Was it because of me or were you too afraid that if you danced alone, your mediocrity would be exposed? Yes, ask yourself your true worth and you will get your answer. Yes, I did cut you off but then you deserved it! So don't come to me saying I destroyed you. I didn't have to. You did it all by yourself. And don't expect me to feel sorry for you, because I'm too busy feeling sorry for myself and Shankar. When he is a little older, he will feel the need for a father. Oh, you will be around all right. Where will you go? But all he will see is your exterior. It won't take him long to realize that *(points to his head)* there's nobody home! *(Moves towards the bedroom.)*

JAIRAJ *(pause, then suddenly)*. If you take the trouble to knock, you'll find someone home. *(Gets up.)* Are you all there for Shankar? He needs you now. Where are you?

RATNA. I know my duties and my capabilities. And I have always taken pride in knowing where I stand.

JAIRAJ. Over there? In that loud costume? Screaming out to everyone 'Here I am'? Is that where you are?

RATNA. That's really fancy, coming from a drunkard like you.

JAIRAJ. No matter how clever an actress you are, you can't convince me that you are playing the part of devoted mother very well. You wouldn't even know where to start.

RATNA. I can start by ending this sick talk with you and feeding the baby. If you have nothing else to say, good night.

JAIRAJ *(scornfully)*. Feeding the baby. That won't be necessary. He is fast asleep. He won't miss his meal.

RATNA. How do you know? He usually wakes up at this hour.

JAIRAJ. Not on the nights you perform.

RATNA. What do you mean?

JAIRAJ. The ayah.

RATNA *(attentively)*. Go on.

JAIRAJ. You wouldn't know. An old trick handed down from one generation of ayahs to the next. I know. I was raised by one.

RATNA *(grimly)*. Opium.

JAIRAJ. Effective, isn't it? He hasn't cried at all. Don't worry, they always give just the right amount.

RATNA *(panicky)*. She too?

JAIRAJ. Yes. She too. She too wants a restful sleep on the kitchen floor, same as her mother and her mother's mother.

RATNA. She too has given . . . Shankar . . . ?

JAIRAJ *(gets up)*. What do you mean?

*A low beat on the mridangam is heard. Ratna looks at him terror-stricken. Jairaj advances towards her.*

What did you say? She too has given Shankar? *(Grabs Ratna.)* What did you say? She too has given Shankar? *(Lets go of her.)* You?

RATNA *(screaming)*. No!

*Jairaj rushes up the stairs. Ratna looks up and slowly goes up the stairs as music plays. The lights dim. She exits hurriedly.*

*The music culminates in a scream which comes from the older Ratna. The garden changes into the living room. The music however continues, perhaps muted. The lights remain subdued. The older Ratna comes down the stairs almost in a trance. The older Jairaj enters, and stands in shadows, watching her as she sits down. He moves and stands beside her. They are both fixed in a spotlight. All sense of time is abandoned now.*

JAIRAJ. It's settled. We move next month. The demolishers will arrive then. They will start with the front. That will be easy to pull down, the new portion. This may be a little more difficult. They made tough buildings in the old days. And tough people. But even tough people like my father get knocked down.

*Spotlight picks up the younger Jairaj and Ratna in the dance hall. They are both in dance costume. Ratna is helping Jairaj with his sash and they both wear their dancing bells during the older Jairaj's speech. They smile a lot and perhaps even laugh.*

We have moved to our flat. A posh flat. Our balcony overlooks the top of a gulmohar tree. They were planning to cut it off, I'm told. It obstructs the traffic. But it was saved by a group of retired old men in this building. I think I was one of them. Did I tell you Lata had called when you had gone to visit Chandra Kala? She was happy to know that you two are the best of friends. I told her how much you two have in common. Arthritis to start with. She called to say that her baby spoke her first word today. It sounded like 'jalebi'.

*The younger Jairaj strikes a pose. The younger Ratna laughs and hits him playfully.*

Today my liver ceased to function. And I followed suit. You died too. Out of boredom, I suspect. Our flat is empty now. It belongs to Lata and Viswas. I see you coming to what seems to be heaven, riding with Death on a buffalo. You get off and I greet you. The buffalo vanishes. *(Flute.)* And we embrace. We smile. And we dance.

*The younger Jairaj and Ratna smile and embrace.*

We dance perfectly. In unison. Not missing a step or a beat. We talk and laugh at all the mistakes we made in our previous dances.

*The younger Ratna strikes a pose which the younger Jairaj seems to disagree with.*

We were only human. We lacked the grace. We lacked the brilliance. We lacked the magic to dance like God.

*The younger couple is ready to dance and salute the audience while the music builds up and the spotlights fade.*